Holidays

MRS. BLALOCK

The TENNESSEE Night Before Christmas

E.J. Sullivan

Illustrated by
Larry Eldredge

SWEETWATER
PRESS

SWEETWATER
PRESS

The Tennessee Night Before Christmas
Copyright © 2005 by Cliff Road Books, Inc.
Produced by arrangement with Sweetwater Press

ISBN-13: 9781581733952
ISBN-10: 1-58173-395-X

Printed in China

The TENNESSEE Night Before Christmas

'Twas a Tennessee night before Christmas,
and from Ruby Falls to Graceland,
Not a creature was stirring – even Dolly's hair
was on its stand.

Our stockings were hung
on the mantel and chimney,
With our musical ornaments
from the Grand Ole Opry.

Baby Sister was snuggled all safe in her bed,
With visions of cheerleader stuff in her head.
And me in my Vols jammies, and Luke in his Titans tee,
Were each of us dreaming of playoff victory.

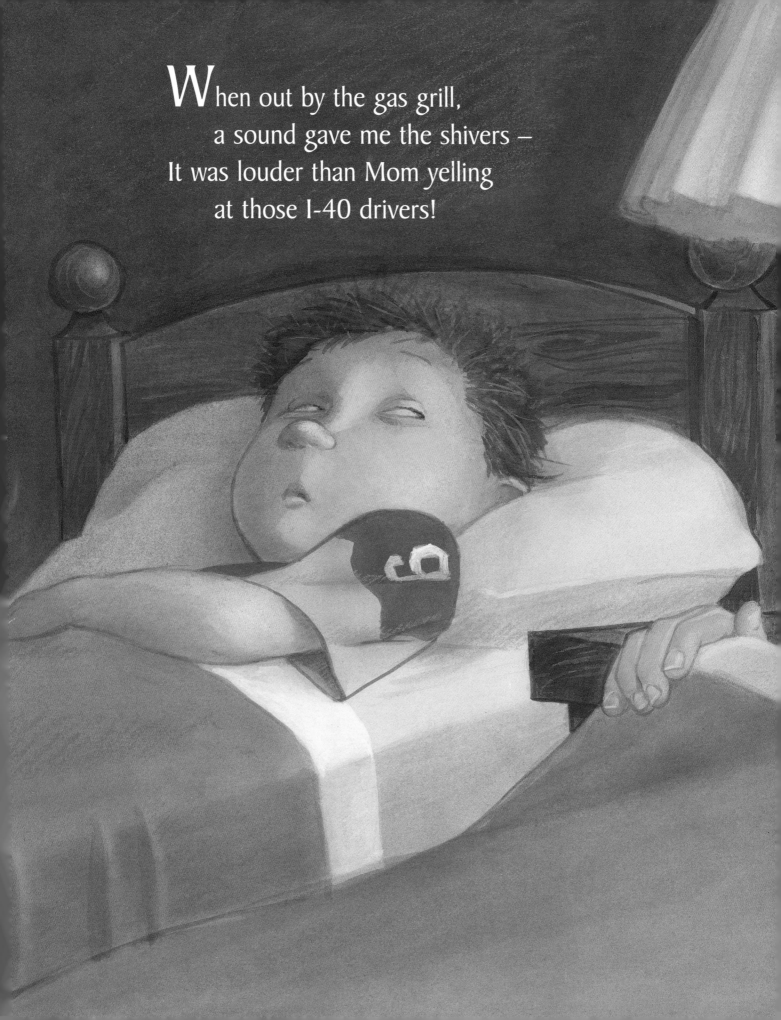

When out by the gas grill,
    a sound gave me the shivers —
It was louder than Mom yelling
    at those I-40 drivers!

I sprang out of bed and ran
down the stair
Armed with Dad's autographed
Hank Jr. guitar!

The moon was as bright as that Cracker Barrel store
They put in down the road – it's open all hours!
And then what to my wondering eyes should I spy
But a country-western band's tour bus flyin' on by!

With a little ol' driver
so lively 'n' quick,
He could'a won the
Bristol 500 in a lick!

Eight musical reindeer were playing along,
And he sang out, so I could hear loud
      and strong:

"Get up Waylon, Willie, Merle, and Johnny C.,
Go Elvis, Loretta, George J., and Tammy!
From Nashville to Memphis and the banks
of the Mississippi –
Now fly up to Knoxville and the peaks of the Smokies!"

You know how in the winter the weathermen go wild,
Saying snow is gonna come and cover us for miles?
That's how crazy I felt watchin' that tour bus sail by —
Got me so worked up I needed an RC and Moon Pie!

As I finished my snack, I saw our redbud tree shake
When the bottom of the Santa bus started to scrape.
I looked up through the limbs and caught him red-handed —
On our Rock City birdhouse Santa'd crash landed!

Bless his heart. He looked wild as Davy Crockett to me,
With his hair and his beard tangled up in that tree.
Mom's always saying I should help folks who are older,
So I helped him get down onto our John Deere mower.

Santa headed inside, stepping over
our dog, Buster,
And filled all our stockings
with Goo Goo Clusters.

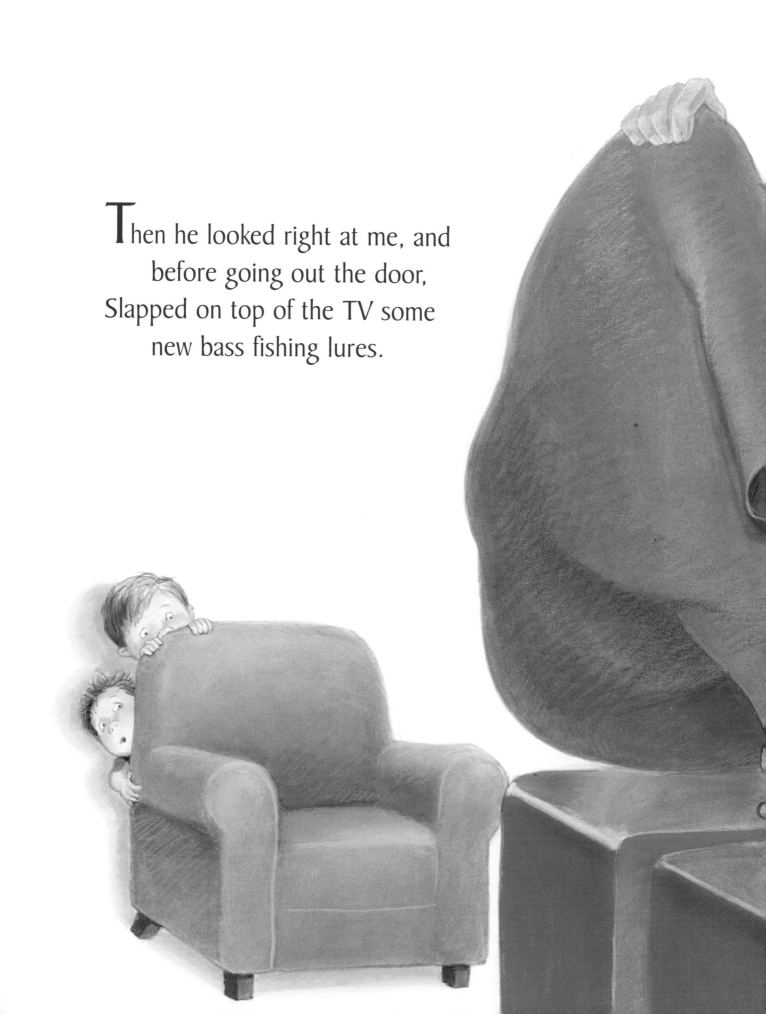

Then he looked right at me, and
before going out the door,
Slapped on top of the TV some
new bass fishing lures.

He fired up the band and soon he was gone,
All the while telling those deer to strum on.
But I heard his refrain as his rig
    sped away,

"Merry Christmas, Tennessee!
I wish I could stay!"